OCTOBER FERRIES TO GABRIOLA

A Radio Play for Five Actors

Praise for
October Ferries to Gabriola

While mixing fact and fiction, Charlotte Cameron concurrently spins the wheel of time backward to 1946 and forward to the present day. In this way, she deftly highlights Malcolm and Margerie Lowry's dream of finding sanctuary and renewal on Gabriola Island while simultaneously illuminating the plight of a similar contemporary couple. Themes such as alcoholism, angst, eviction and homelessness, guilt, hope, and love reverberate throughout this provocative drama.

Sheryl Salloum, author of
Malcolm Lowry: Vancouver Days

Playwright Charlotte Cameron has taken Malcolm Lowry's unfinished novel, *October Ferry to Gabriola*, a barely fictional account of his and his second wife's visit to the island, as a theme for his pursuit of an ideal place both for creativity and redemption. Cameron cleverly overlaps Lowry's story with that of a similar, but contemporary couple—both alcoholic husbands with a guilt in their past and desperately supportive wives. Her brilliant dialogue, as in all good dramas, raises questions about possible redemption and this never-ending quest of ours for Paradise on Earth.

Naomi Beth Wakan, Inaugural Poet Laureate
of Nanaimo and author of *On the Arts*

OCTOBER FERRIES TO GABRIOLA

A Radio Play for Five Actors

by

Charlotte Cameron

FICTIVE PRESS

A FICTIVE PRESS Book

Copyright © 2017 by Charlotte Cameron.

All rights reserved. This book or any portion thereof may not be reproduced or used in any manner whatsoever without the express written permission of the publisher, except for brief quotations in a book review or scholarly journal.

While the events described and some of the characters in the play may be based on actual historical events and real people, the play is a work of fiction.

A First Fictive Press Edition.

First published in 2017 by Fictive Press, a division of BizNet Communications (2815699 Canada Inc.), British Columbia, Canada.

fictivepress.com

"Fictive Press" and "fictivepress.com" are trademarks of 2815699 Canada Inc.

Amateur rights: Playwrights Guild of Canada administers amateur rights (for schools, community groups and amateur theatre group). Details at http://www.playwrightsguild.ca/services-visitors

Professional rights: Contact Fictive Press at publish@fictivepress.com

Cover design by Fictive Press. Cover photo of the Atrevida ferry, courtesy of the Gabriola Historical & Museum Society. Author photo by Tom Cameron.

Quotation from a postcard written by Malcolm Lowry, mentioned in *Malcolm Lowry: Vancouver Days*, Sheryl Salloum, Harbour Publishing, 1987, www.harbourpublishing.com

Library and Archives Canada Cataloguing in Publication

Cameron, Charlotte, author
October ferries to Gabriola : a radio play for five actors / Charlotte Cameron.

Issued in print and electronic formats.

ISBN 978-1-927663-55-4 (softcover).--ISBN 978-1-927663-56-1 (ebook).
--ISBN 978-1-927663-57-8 (Kindle).--ISBN 978-1-927663-58-5 (PDF)

I. Title.

PS8605.A47885O28 2017	C812'.6	C2017-900927-3
		C2017-900928-1

*For my husband, Tom Cameron,
for always lifting up my heart.*

Contents

Foreword i
    The Dreamed-of Place by Phyllis Reeve i

Introduction 1
    My Fascination with Malcolm Lowry 1

October Ferries to Gabriola 5
    Synopsis 5
    Production Directions 6
    Main Characters 6
    Minor Characters 6
    Setting 7
    Props 7
    Costumes 8

October Ferries to Gabriola Act One 9

October Ferries to Gabriola Act Two 47

About the Author 77

Acknowledgements 79

Foreword

The Dreamed-of Place

by Phyllis Reeve

*"Gabriola! Ah, if it should prove the right place ...
the dreamed-of place."*

With this thought, Ethan and Jacqueline Llewellyn, the protagonists of Malcolm Lowry's final novel, *October Ferry to Gabriola*, anticipate their arrival on the island. We do not know whether Gabriola was the "right place" for the Llewellyns; the book ends before the ferry docks. Nor can we know whether it could have been the right place for Malcolm and Margerie Lowry. They did arrive, but after a day or two, they re-embarked on the ferries to the Mainland and never returned.

For playwright Charlotte Cameron, as for myself, Gabriola Island turned out to be the right place. We sought a change of direction that would be also a continuation of our lives. The Gabriola ferry brought us to our next chapter.

The ferry that brings the Llewellyns towards the island carries ominous suggestions of Charon's ferry, which in Greek mythology carried souls to Hades. Like their author, the Llewellyns come from a dark place and carry heavy personal baggage. Circumstances worked against the Lowrys' return to Gabriola, but the circumstances were as much internal as external, less a desire to go "home" to Britain than a reluctance to commit or submit to whatever it was that Gabriola symbolized for Lowry.

Enter Cameron's *dramatis personae*, Edward and Sarah, a Millennial couple who use laptops instead of typewriters but who bear their own heavy fardels toward that undiscovered country known to Hamlet—and to Lowry. The fictional characters are more than mere doppelgangers for the Lowrys, but there are enough parallels to give them pause as they examine and even relive the events leading to Malcolm's death. Suicide? Murder? Death by misadventure? Edward's exclamation "We're going to Paradise" is distressing. Paradise can be final. At the same time, Edward wants to take care of unfinished business and protests that he does not want to be a "zombie." The play progresses as a life-against-death struggle and an attempted repudiation of guilt.

Probably, Lowry did not deliberately leave *October Ferry to Gabriola* as an unfinished draft, but his doing so seems more significant the more one ponders it. Gabriola may be the *dreamed-of* place but not necessarily the *right* place. Edward and Sarah have to work this out. Is the island a retreat or a way forward? Which was it for Malcolm and Margerie, and which is it for them? Charlotte Cameron sweeps us up and carries us along into their quest. As we walk the beach on Gabriola and imagine Lowry's cry for help, we will the island to become a symbol of hope.

> *Phyllis Reeve has written books and essays on local and personal history, and hosted the 1994 symposium, "Malcolm Lowry's October Ferry; a Gabriola Island Tribute," on Gabriola Island, where she has resided for thirty years. She is currently a contributing editor to* The *Dorchester Review.*

Introduction

My Fascination with Malcolm Lowry

When my husband, Tom Cameron, and I were looking for a Gulf Island home in British Columbia, we stayed at a Bed & Breakfast on Gabriola Island, where I spotted Malcolm Lowry's novel, *October Ferry to Gabriola,* on a bookshelf. Although I was familiar with his famous work, *Under the Volcano*, I hadn't heard of this novel, which Lowry never completed. I identified with the couple's search for a home, and when we finally found our place on Gabriola, I was curious to learn about Lowry's visit to our island.

I was already a fan of the quarterly *BC BookWorld*, which frequently mentioned Lowry. Its publisher/editor, Alan Twigg, has made a huge contribution to the Lowry story, even organizing a bus tour, "The Malcolm Lowry Brown Bag Mystery Literary Tour," in Vancouver during Expo 86. In 2016, Twigg put Malcolm Lowry on *BC BookWorld's* interactive "Literary Map of BC."

After moving to Gabriola in 2005, I soon discovered that Malcolm Lowry had a following on the island. Phyllis Reeve and her husband, the late Ted Reeve, had hosted a Malcolm Lowry event at their Pages Resort & Marina, in 1994. Phyllis's edited excerpts of the presentations were subsequently published in *Malcolm Lowry's October Ferry: A Gabriola Island Tribute* (The Sandstone Studio, Page's Resort & Marina, and Reference West, 1996).

From Sheryl Salloum's biography, *Malcolm Lowry: Vancouver Days* (Harbour Publishing Co. Ltd., 1987), I learned that Salloum had visited Gabriola in 1985, where she interviewed Alfred McKee, the husband of Margerie Lowry's friend, Angela McKee. McKee's recollections are one of the few documented records of the Lowrys' visit to Gabriola.

I sensed there might be a play in all of this, but cautioned myself against jumping into the story. After writing two historical plays, which were performed at the Edmonton International Fringe Theatre Festival in 2000 and 2001, I knew it would be a challenge to attempt a play about Lowry. However, in 2005, I submitted a 10-minute play about Lowry to a playwriting contest and then forgot all about it. One day, the contest organizer phoned. Although I didn't win, he wanted me to know that the judges felt I was working on something worthwhile. Encouragement like this means a lot to a writer.

In 2008, I learned that the Atrevida, the ferry the Lowrys had taken to Gabriola in 1946, had been converted into a floating bakery off Galiano Island. Tom and I kayaked from Gabriola to Galiano, where we camped at Montague Harbour Provincial Park. We paddled out to the bakery and were invited to look around. It was exciting to be on the very ferry where the Lowrys had once stood, imagining what it would have been like in 1946.

Lowry had a photographic memory, which is reflected in his descriptions of the ferry in *October Ferry to Gabriola*. Although the book is fiction, he likely described actual passengers, as well as the signs and posters he read before boarding.

I continued to follow in Lowry's footsteps. In 2011, Tom and I travelled to Mexico, where Margerie and Malcolm lived from December 1945 until May 1946. In Cuernavaca, we saw the small living quarters on the hotel's roof, where we were told they wrote. We imagined Malcolm enjoying himself in the hotel's swimming pool.

We walked along Calle Humbolt, pausing at the wall in front of number 62, the house where Lowry lived in 1936 and 1937 with his first wife, Jan Gabrial, the model for Yvonne in *Under the Volcano* and author of *Inside the Volcano*: *My Life with Malcolm Lowry* (St. Martin's Press, New York, 2000).

We took a guided tour into the deep, winding *barranca*. Being there made it easy to understand how the now-fenced ravine featured so dramatically in *Under the Volcano.* We went by bus to Oaxaca, as the Lowrys had done. From a rooftop in Mexico City, we could glimpse Popocatépetl and Ixtaccihuatl, the volcanoes Lowry made famous in his masterpiece.

For inspiration, I've repeatedly watched the 1984 Hollywood movie, *Under the Volcano,* and the 1976 National Film Board of Canada documentary, *Volcano: An Inquiry into the Life and Death of Malcolm Lowry*.

Two scholarly editions of Lowry's letters, *Sursum Corda! The Collected Letters of Malcolm Lowry* (University of Toronto Press, 1995, 1996) by University of British Columbia English professor Sherrill Grace helped me understand Lowry better. *Sersum Corda!*—lift up your hearts, in Latin—is how Lowry often signed his letters.

I found it hard to read accounts of Lowry when he was down and out. Alcoholism was a central reality of his life, and he had many other problems. He made mistakes, but his friends stuck with him. They didn't always like his behaviour, but they took him in and tried to help him.

Lowry also had many good points. This was confirmed by Gloria Levi, a woman I met by chance in the summer of

2016. Levi had lived near the Lowrys at Dollarton in the early 1950s and thought that Lowry deserved more recognition for being a kind, sensitive person, a good neighbour and friend. Levi graciously agreed to have her Lowry memories recorded on video for posterity.

That same year, I became involved in the 70th anniversary celebration of the Lowrys' visit to Gabriola. As part of the festivities, my radio play, *October Ferries to Gabriola,* was performed in October 2016 at Surf Lodge, where the Lowrys had stayed. Earlier versions of the play had been performed on Gabriola as a reading at the Roxy Theatre in 2009, at the Poetry Gabriola Festival at Dragon's Lodge in 2010 and at the Islands Study Conference in 2013. With each draft, the play evolved, sometimes getting lighter, sometimes darker.

Since the play's October 2016 performances, people have asked me about Lowry's mysterious "death by misadventure" in 1957. No one knows for sure how he died. "Malcolm Lowry's Mysterious Demise," an article in *The New Yorker* (December, 2007), raised many questions but came to no definitive conclusions. Lowry was only 46 when he died.

In spite of all the articles and books written about Malcolm Lowry, scholars continue to visit the University of British Columbia's Rare Books and Special Collections to study Lowry's handwriting, letters, photographs, novels, poems and short stories. It appears that I am not alone in my fascination with Malcolm Lowry—one that shows no signs of abating.

Charlotte Cameron
Gabriola Island, BC

October Ferries to Gabriola

Synopsis

This play is an act of imagination, inspired by the life of Malcolm Lowry, who wrote his masterpiece, *Under the Volcano*, mainly in British Columbia (Canada) and Mexico.

In 1946, Malcolm Lowry and his wife, Margerie, arrived by ferry on Gabriola Island in British Columbia, hoping to find a home where they could live, love and write.

This play juxtaposes the lives of the Lowrys with the lives of a contemporary couple, writer Edward Jones and his singer/songwriter wife, Sarah Smith. Sarah and Edward also catch an October ferry to Gabriola, hoping to escape their troubles and start a new life. But they are haunted by the Lowrys.

A note of hopefulness at the end of the play gives the audience an opportunity to imagine how life could have been better for Malcolm and Margerie if they had stayed on Gabriola.

Enigmatic storyteller Jan Gabrial, Lowry's first wife, begins the play with a short monologue about her perceived image of islands as delightful, magical places. Other monologues by Gabrial act as a bridge between scenes with the Lowrys and those with Edward and Sarah.

Production Directions

This play can be produced as a traditional radio play, for an audio-only audience. It can also be staged as a live performance, with costumed actors manipulating the special effects behind a table, and moving around the stage to deliver their lines.

Main Characters

JAN GABRIAL (1911–2001), Lowry's first wife

MALCOLM LOWRY (1909–1957), writer

MARGERIE LOWRY (1905–1988), Lowry's second wife

EDWARD JONES, a contemporary academic

SARAH SMITH, singer/songwriter, Jones's wife

Minor Characters

Narrator

Manservant at Surf Lodge

Earle Birney, Canadian poet

Bus driver

Man on ferry

Male psychiatrist #1

Male psychiatrist #2

Setting

The action takes place in a variety of locales: Hollywood, California; Dollarton and Gabriola Island, British Columbia; Mexico; and England. Transitions between scenes are handled with music and sound effects, which are also used to punctuate the action.

Props

A large pill bottle filled with tiny candies that rattle.

Lowry's novel, October Ferry to Gabriola.

A bottle of gin.

Cigarettes.

Newspapers.

Envelopes.

Dice.

Postcards.

A ukulele.

Bracelets hanging on a string near the microphone.

A typewriter with paper.

A filter to muffle voices.

A tinkling bell to indicate that the scene is imaginary.

A rotary telephone.

Pieces of glass.

Laptop computer.

Bag of baseballs, cushions, etc. to mimic the sound of a body falling when dropped.

Costumes

If the play is produced as a live stage performance, Margerie and Jan should have a glamorous 1940s look. Margerie should wear a fur coat when she and Malcolm catch the ferry to Gabriola. Malcolm should wear appropriate 1940s clothing, including a wool overcoat when on the ferry.

Sarah and Edward should be dressed in contemporary clothing. Since the actors also play the minor roles, glasses, jackets, and other accessories should indicate who they are.

October Ferries to Gabriola

Act One

SOUND: Stravinsky opera plays for 15 sec., then stops.

NARRATOR: Welcome to Surf Lodge on beautiful Gabriola Island in British Columbia.

Imagine! Malcolm Lowry and his wife Margerie were here in 1946, in this very room. Lowry had just finished his famous novel, *Under the Volcano*. They were searching for a new home because they feared they would soon be evicted from their shack in Dollarton. They hoped that on Gabriola, they might find a place to live, love and write.

Now imagine a contemporary couple in [today's year], almost a mirror image of the Lowrys, stuck in a personal quagmire, seeking refuge on Gabriola. Will they be able to find what they are looking for?

Stay tuned, hold on tight, and get ready for a rollercoaster ride full of surprises, including the appearance of Jan Gabrial, Lowry's first wife. She starts things off for us with her version of the story.

TRANSITION: Stravinsky opera music.

JAN: Jan Gabrial isn't my real name. It's my stage name. The one I used when I met Malcolm, and I've kept it. (Comparing) Gabrial, Gabriola, Gabrial, Gabriola.

Imagine! Gabriola is a real island! When I saw the title of Malcolm's book, *October Ferry to Gabriola*, I was sure it was an imaginary place he had dreamed up and named after me. I realized my mistake when I looked in an atlas and found the island near Vancouver. Malcolm would have considered it a coincidence. He couldn't get over the fact that he'd named the main character in *Ultramarine*, Janet, years before he met me. Poor Malcolm! An island must be magical. I wish he'd found peace there.

SOUND: Seagulls crying, ukulele flow.

JAN: We met in Spain in 1933. I was twenty-two and he was twenty-four. I should have listened to the little voice telling me to keep away from him. But he was romantic, witty and funny. He insisted we get married in Paris. In spite of myself, I gave in. As my wedding gift, he gave me two ukuleles!

SOUND: Ukulele sting.

JAN: Oh, I knew our life was going to be all about him. After our divorce, I was glad to hear he'd found someone to help him. He was lucky to have met Margerie at that bus stop in L.A.

TRANSITION: Footsteps on pavement. Stop. Cigarette being lit.

NARRATOR: Los Angeles. 1940.

LOWRY: Hello. I saw you in the theatre. Did you come alone?

MARG: Yes. I didn't want to miss the film. What did you think of it?

LOWRY: It was rather mellifluously melodious for my taste. (Chuckles) How about you?

MARG: Um. Yes. Well, I have to say the death scene was melodramatic. I could have done it better.

LOWRY: Really? Are you an actress?

SOUND: Bracelets jingling.

MARG: (Nods enthusiastically) Uh huh.

LOWRY: Professional or amateur?

MARG: Professional.

LOWRY: I don't believe I've seen your work. If I had, I would have remembered you.

MARG: Don't you watch Westerns?

LOWRY: Sometimes ... Why? Are you the horse?

SOUND: Beat of dead silence.

LOWRY: (Laughs) I'm sorry. That was inexcusably rude of me. I was just trying to break the ice.

MARG: Apology accepted. I'm usually the cowgirl.

LOWRY: Isn't that rather dangerous?

MARG: Not for a champion rider!

LOWRY: And what do you do when you're not living dangerously?

MARG: I'm the "personal assistant" on the set of *Blondie*. That's my forte!

LOWRY: How interesting. I should have introduced myself. I'm Malcolm Lowry.

MARG: I'm Margerie Bonner and I confess I know who you are. Someone pointed you out to me. I'm reading *Ultramarine.* It's fascinating! Did you really take that sea voyage?

LOWRY: Yes I did, but the book's all fiction.

MARG: (Laughs) That's what you writers always say, but I know better. It must have been something else to plough through a storm with all those animals. I wouldn't have survived!

LOWRY: I've a feeling you would have done just fine.

MARG: You were a prodigy, with a novel published so young.

LOWRY: Not really. I was twenty-four and I didn't do much else at Cambridge except read, write and go to the cinema.

MARG: Well, I'm impressed.

LOWRY: I was lucky. My manuscript was stolen from my editor's car, but a friend found an earlier draft in the trash.

MARG: Oh my! That was lucky. The word is out in Hollywood that you're doing a screenplay.

SOUND: Bracelets jingling.

MARG: Any role for me?

LOWRY: I'm just the writer. But perhaps you could show me around before I leave for Canada. L.A. is such a change from Mexico!

MARG: Well, I've got a convertible. My cheetah likes to ride in the backseat.

LOWRY: You're pulling my leg! The convertible sounds like fun but ...

MARG: (Fast) The cheetah's fun, too. She's tame. Don't worry darling, I'll keep her in her cage! Hey, maybe I could help you with that screenplay! I'm a writer too, you know. Are you still married?

LOWRY: Do you always ask so many beastly questions? If you must know, my divorce has just settled.

MARG: So, maybe it's for the best. What did your ex do?

LOWRY: She writes. Jan Gabrial.

MARG: Never heard of her.

LOWRY: No? And like you, she's an actress. It's quite a coincidence when you think about it.

MARG: Oh, so you're thinking about it!

SOUND: Bus arriving.

LOWRY: Here's the bus. (Pause) After you.

SOUND: Bus leaving. Pause.

TRANSITION: Ferry horn.

NARRATOR: We find ourselves in Nanaimo, British Columbia, in October [today's year].

SOUND: Ukulele flow.

SARAH: Oh, Ed, we'll be fine. We'll have a little cottage by the sea where we can write and write! Just like we planned.

EDWARD: You can write your songs anywhere, but I've abandoned everything. I don't know why I didn't finish my thesis. I know *all* about Malcolm Lowry. Why did I quit?

SARAH: Why did you?

EDWARD: (Shrugs) All that work and I have nothing.

SARAH: You do have something. Us. Look at the Lowrys. They lost everything in that fire. Why don't you write to your advisor?

Maybe she'll give you a second chance. I'll help you.

EDWARD: We'll see.

SARAH: It'll be better for us here. We'll start a new life. (Pause) Gabriola is called the Isle of the Arts. We'll fit in. Blackberries grow wild there! I'll bake pies and sell them by the side of the road!

EDWARD: Who'll buy them? You don't even know how to bake. I need a drink!

SARAH: (Emphatically) You don't need a drink! I'm going down to the dock, to that payphone.

EDWARD: Who're you going to phone?

SARAH: The Hopes! Don't you think it's nice of them to put us up until we find our place?

SOUND: Female footsteps, gin in paper bag being drunk. Snoring.

SOUND: Female footsteps on pavement.

SARAH: Wake up, Ed. I like it here already. People are so friendly! They know about

Lowry. Surf Lodge was actually called Anderson Lodge when the Lowrys were here. Oh, and the Hopes will meet the ferry. We'll be on Gabriola before dark.

EDWARD: You make it sound like Paradise.

SARAH: It could be. Give it a chance. Lowry's haunting you. It has to be better than that awful basement suite in Toronto. We had to move. We had no choice after the fire.

EDWARD: Yeah. Just like Lowry's shack burst into flames.

SARAH: At least that's their story. Margerie saved the manuscript.

EDWARD: Lowry couldn't get the fire out of his head.

SARAH: At least he talked about his troubles. (Pause) It might help if you did that. Accidents happen. I know it's hard for you, being the survivor. But it wasn't your fault. You weren't drinking.

EDWARD: I was, actually. My wife died. It was my fault.

SARAH: You weren't driving. (Pause) I'm going to run up to the mall and get flowers for the Hopes.

EDWARD: Coals to Newcastle.

SARAH: Oh, Ed. This is the start of a new life. We're honeymooners!

EDWARD: I don't like honeymoons.

SARAH: Don't be cruel! (Sniffing) Do I smell gin?

EDWARD: Yeah. So?

SOUND: Gin in paper bag being drunk.

SARAH: Listen. Do you want to end up like Lowry? You're not him. He was hardly ever sober. (Pause) Maybe you should see a doctor.

EDWARD: Or get hypnotized. Whatever.

SARAH: Whatever happened, we can turn it around. You aren't an alcoholic. Lowry was an alcoholic by the time he was eighteen. He had terrible parents. Yours are great. (Pause) You never told them why you quit, did you?

EDWARD: I told them I wasn't going to finish my thesis because of the car accident.

SARAH: I don't think you did anything wrong, not like Lowry. He plagiarized! He copied out lines from Jan Gabrial's letters, not that he worried about it—she was just his wife. Didn't you say he had a photographic memory? Maybe that's what happened to you?

EDWARD: People stole from Lowry. Jan took ideas from him.

SARAH: Your thesis argues against ownership. Your parents would have understood. You know, they've always been supportive. They've always treated you like a prince.

EDWARD: Aren't you Miss Goody Two Shoes? Why don't you take a walk or something?

SARAH: That sounds like "take a hike." Fine! Goody Two Shoes has time to go to the mall. Can I get you something?

SOUND: Female footsteps.

EDWARD: Like more to drink?

SOUND: Footsteps stop.

SARAH: (Pause) As if. Anyway, watch out! Lowry's wives were both writers and so am I. Songwriting rules.

SOUND: Ukulele sting.

EDWARD: Good-bye.

SOUND: Female footsteps.

TRANSITION: Music from the 1940s.

SOUND: Typing on a typewriter and paper being pulled out.

NARRATOR: It is summer, 1945. The Lowrys are in a shack on Dollarton Beach, British Columbia.

SOUND: Typing on a typewriter and paper being pulled out.

MARG: My novel is coming along nicely. Time for a short break. (Pause) Malcolm, you should sit. Your legs are suffering, and your poor hands!

LOWRY: I can't sit. It hurts too much.

MARG: Here. Take some of these painkillers the doctor gave you. That's what they're for.

SOUND: Pill bottle rattling, then opening.

LOWRY: I've failed at everything. I couldn't even stop our home from burning down!

MARG: You have to forget it. Quit reliving it. We got another cabin here in Dollarton. We've been lucky.

LOWRY: I'm not as sanguine as you. I couldn't have stood it if we'd had to move back to bloody, dreary Enochsvilleport!

MARG: (Laughs) Is that what you're calling Vancouver now? I like it there. It's a good place for us.

LOWRY: It's better here. We're with friends.

MARG: We had lots of friends in Vancouver. I like Dollarton too. But I didn't marry you to live my life in a shack.

LOWRY: I don't believe I married you under false pretenses. (Joking) I know you couldn't be after my vast fortune.

MARG: (Shakes her bracelets) Well, now we can look on the bright side. We escaped the fire. I saved your manuscript!

SOUND: Papers rustling.

LOWRY: I wouldn't have recovered if I'd lost it.

MARG: We just have to buckle down.

LOWRY: I should have been a poet. Here's something for my tombstone.

SOUND: Paper being passed. Rustling.

MARG: (Reads) *"Malcolm Lowry, Late of the Bowery, His prose was flowery and often glowery. He lived nightly and drank daily and died playing the ukulele."*

SOUND: Ukulele sting.

MARG: (Nicely) I don't think so Malcolm. Every line of your novel is poetry! Just finish it. We are in the perfect place to do it.

LOWRY: Yes. The ocean, the path to the spring, and peace.

MARG: Of course, some people would say we are missing necessities, like a library, running water and a fire department.

LOWRY: Our friends are helping us. We should build a pier! Make this place our own.

MARG: We're just squatters. We'll be evicted sooner or later. (Pause) But what the hell, let's seize the moment and build a crazy pier. Just one thing, though. Your manuscript is now longer, even though I suggested making it shorter. You made it denser.

LOWRY: Deeper.

MARG: This is the fourth draft. All you need to do is get rid of the Consul's wife.

LOWRY: (Laughs) And the Consul, don't forget.

MARG: You could have her killed by a horse. I know about horses.

LOWRY: I'll consider it. We should go to Mexico this fall, now that the inheritance from my old man is coming through. (Beat of silence) I'd like to show you around. Soak up more atmosphere.

MARG: I thought you just said you wanted to stay here. You don't need to soak up anything more.

LOWRY: (Laughs) Then it'll be for the sequel, *Under, Under the Volcano*. Let's go for a swim.

MARG: Oh you goof. I'll join you in a bit. I might as well get back to my book, since we aren't getting anything done on yours.

LOWRY: Right. I'll wash the windows while I wait for you. I feel like a god when I'm washing windows.

SOUND: Washing windows.

LOWRY: (Shouts) *"Wonders are many and none is more wonderful than man."*

MARG: That's beautiful. You are a genius.

LOWRY: That's Sophocles. *He* was a genius. It'll be the epigraph at the beginning of the book. There's no copyright on that quote.

SOUND: Typing and paper being pulled out. New sheet of paper being put in.

MARG: Malc, (beat of silence) I've been wanting to ask why you haven't talked about your father's death. Your "old man," as you call him. (Pause)

SOUND: Distant ocean.

MARG: I understand it must have been hard for you but, really, you scared me when you swam out so far.

LOWRY: I like swimming.

MARG: It was February.

LOWRY: I'd rather not discuss my father. But, I wasn't trying to commit suicide, as you seemed to think. (Emphatically) I'm not a quitter, Margerie.

MARG: Well. You should be nicer to your mother. Write to her once in a while.

LOWRY: Why? Nice? That's an appalling proposition. She didn't even want me to come home during a school holiday when I had that eye infection. She couldn't stand to look at me.

MARG: It wouldn't hurt to write.

LOWRY: Just to warn you, I have moments of darkness. More than moments. I was cruel and violent with Jan.

MARG: I can't see you being violent, Malcolm.

LOWRY: I punched a horse right in the face once. It fell down dead.

SOUND: Punch, neigh, fall.

MARG: Surely not dead.

LOWRY: Very close.

MARG: Your tongue can be cruel but you feel bad afterwards. You got help when you checked yourself into Bellevue Hospital.

LOWRY: I was attempting a cure for my (makes quoting gesture with fingertips) "drunkenness." Also, I was after material for a story.

MARG: Do I know about this? Did you publish a story based on that experience?

LOWRY: Yes. It was accepted for publication but I changed my mind. I wanted to do more work on it.

SOUND: Bracelets jingling.

MARG: (Rolls her eyes) Oh, of course.

LOWRY: Then I agreed to have it published in a French magazine. Just to prove copyright.

MARG: What was it called? Were the patients crazy?

LOWRY: Not as crazy as the outside world. And the doctor was nice. He might have cured me if the Americans hadn't kicked me out because I was a foreigner. "Lunar Caustic." That's what I called it.

MARG: Well. Whatever it's called, I hope you are cured. Going to Mexico will be a way to find out. To prove to yourself, and to me, that you're better. It would be good to be somewhere warm for the winter. I'd just love to see those volcanoes! (Pause) But before we go, I want the satisfaction of putting *Under* in the mail. And you have to promise not to start drinking again.

LOWRY: You drive a hard bargain, Margerie, my dear.

TRANSITION: Accordion music.

JAN: I should have left him before our wedding. Especially after what happened on New Year's Eve in Paris. I wanted to go to a party, but Malcolm wanted to stay home with me. We should have remained alone. As soon as we got to the party, he started drinking. Then he disappeared. When he came back, he caught me dancing to accordion music. He yelled insults at me and hit my dance partner. It was not pretty.

SOUND: Smack, loud thud.

JAN: I left in shame, with murmurs of "How can she marry him?" echoing in my head. Whatever possessed me to go ahead and marry him? I had plenty of reasons to call it quits. He was jealous of my male friends and didn't even want his father to meet me. Malcolm said his "old man" would cut him off if he knew about me. He read my diary and accused me of promiscuity. Three months after our wedding in Paris, I left him and took off for New York.

Changing countries didn't solve the problem. Malcolm was a charming letter writer and his words seduced me into giving him another chance. Initially, he charmed my mother, but she soon discovered his problem. When I had to be hospitalized because Malcolm bit my breast and an infection set in, it broke her heart, not so much that he bit me as that he didn't even visit me in the hospital. Then he told me he wanted to live alone. I got an apartment and a job in a dancehall. When I heard Malcolm was in the psychiatric ward at Bellevue, I knew I had to get him out.

VOICES: Help me. Please. Help! Mommy. Don't hit me. Help! Etc.

JAN: (Speaking over voices) He was frightened. I told the hospital he wasn't an American, and he was free, just like that. (Voices stop) They didn't want to keep him. Neither did I. But I was stuck with him. When I heard Mexico was cheap, we took a long trip across America by bus.

SOUND: Bus noises.

JAN: All the way to California, and then by boat to Mexico, arriving on the Day of the Dead.

SOUND: Mexican music.

JAN: We rented a house with a garden in Cuernavaca and Malcolm started writing *Under the Volcano*. I was the model for Yvonne. I was his muse. He incorporated me into his novel in so many ways. We were happy: living, loving and writing.

SOUND: Exotic bird calls.

JAN: We were calm, but when his old friends showed up for a drink ... (Throws up her hands).

SOUND: People drinking and laughing.

ACTORS: Hey there, have another one on me. Just one for the road, etc.

JAN: I went back to the States and applied for a divorce. I didn't get a settlement, but Malcolm inherited a fortune when his mother died. When I phoned him after the success of *Under the Volcano* ...

SOUND: Telephone rings. Phone picked up.

LOWRY: (Speaking through filter) Hello.

MARG: Hang up that phone!

SOUND: Phone slams down.

JAN: Maybe Margerie was jealous of me. Maybe she thought I was trying to cash in on Malcolm's fame. (Shrugs) I'm one of the few people to have the strange experience of reading numerous biographies about my "ex" and his second wife. One thing I know is that when he took Margerie to Mexico, it was a disaster.

TRANSITION: Acoustic guitar. Street noises.

SOUND: Envelope rustles.

LOWRY: (Groans) I can't open these letters.

SOUND: Door opens, body falls, female footsteps.

MARG: What's wrong with you? How can you just lie under that table, doing nothing? The least you could have done was pay that fine instead of being so high and mighty with the Mexican authorities.

SOUND: Scuffling to indicate struggling to stand up.

LOWRY: It's too late now. I'm not allowed to do anything. Those *vaqueros* are watching this place. It was bad enough to be thrown in jail, for no reason. But, to be forbidden to write! I can't even write a letter to my mother!

MARG: Drunk and disorderly behavior is a reason. You're worse than ever. It was your idea to come to Mexico, so quit complaining. What a mess! I've been through hell trying to explain to the British Consul how we lost our passports. Now we need pictures to get new ones. And it gets worse. You're going to be deported, and me along with you, because our tourist cards say we're writers and we don't have work permits. Tomorrow, we'll be in jail. (Beat of silence) Are you listening? In jail! While I was running around all over Mexico on that filthy old bus, you were here in Cuernavaca drinking. You promised you wouldn't. (Weeping) I'm so tired I could kill myself.

LOWRY: Go ahead. That's what my old schoolmate said and he did it too.

MARG: You don't mean that. You felt guilty for not stopping him. His suicide still haunts you. (Pause) If only we hadn't come here.

LOWRY: This is where I need to be. Jonathan Cape's reader was so inexorably critical, I almost gave up. I have to be here to write.

MARG: They'd have let you off if you'd given them *mordida*.

LOWRY: I'm not paying them a cent. They don't like me. They think I'm a spy.

MARG: Don't make yourself sound glamorous. You don't have to be a genius to realize the things you've written about Mexico aren't exactly complimentary. (Pause) What are you staring at? Here, give me those envelopes.

LOWRY: Crap! Don't open them. More bloody rejections. I need a drink. Margerie, help me.

MARG: Sure. I'll get you a drink. I'll borrow the money.

LOWRY: No, don't leave me. I'm sorry. Open the letters.

SOUND: Envelope ripping, paper being pulled out.

MARG: Oh, Malcolm!

LOWRY: (At a loss) What is it?

MARG: It's the opposite of rejection. Your novel has been accepted by both publishers. By Jonathan Cape. And they say they won't ask for a single revision. And Reynal and Hitchcock will accept it as is. Oh Malc! (Delighted) This does call for a drink. I'll be right back.

SOUND: Female footsteps. Door closes.

LOWRY: (Reads aloud) *"Dear Mr. Lowry, It is with great pleasure that we at Jonathan Cape inform you that we will publish Under the Volcano. Your long letter of January 2nd, 1946 has convinced us that, although the novel begins slowly it is not tedious. As you said, the book needs to be read and reread ..."*

SOUND: Door opens. Female footsteps.

MARG: What was I thinking? I remembered I had this bottle of tequila in the closet.

LOWRY: They sent the letters to the wrong address. That's why we didn't hear anything. It's too late.

MARG: It's not too late. They can't keep us in jail. They'll have to let us go. Then we can walk across the border and we're out of here.

LOWRY: But where will we live?

MARG: Don't start worrying. We'll think of something.

LOWRY: Maybe we could buy an island.

SOUND: Bracelets jingling.

MARG: We'll find a place. A place where we can be happy. Where you can write all you like. I'll help you. Sometimes I think you married me for my editing.

LOWRY: No, it was your typing. (They laugh weakly.)

TRANSITION: A ferry horn.

NARRATOR: Edward and Sarah's cottage on Gabriola Island.

SOUND: Ukulele flow.

SARAH: (Humming) *Love Letters in the Sand*.

SOUND: Door opening.

EDWARD: Hello.

SARAH: How was your appointment?

EDWARD: It was a start. The doctor gives good advice. He says I'm depressed, but I told him I don't want to take drugs. I don't want to be a zombie.

SARAH: So, it went well?

EDWARD: Yeah. He thinks he can help me out of this depression.

SARAH: That's good

EDWARD: He thinks I should ask for a second chance.

SARAH: That's what I think also.

EDWARD: Also, he said I should start by telling you the whole story.

SARAH: Well, I'm listening.

EDWARD: (Speaking slowly) You remember the day of the accident. Amber and I walked by your apartment. It was cold, but you were sitting on the balcony playing your ukulele.

SOUND: Cheerful ukulele flow.

You were wearing those gloves with the ends of the fingers cut off. You told us you were celebrating a royalty cheque. I said I'd turned in my thesis and was going to give a talk at a conference.

SARAH: You both looked fabulous. All dressed up and happy.

EDWARD: Too happy, I guess. Pride goes before a fall. At the conference, I acknowledged the support of my beautiful wife and said she was working on a thesis about Dylan Thomas. Later, the questions started. How could I be so sure that Dylan Thomas changed the title of his play to *Under Milkwood* as a way of tipping his hat to Lowry's masterpiece, *Under the Volcano*? Then I gave away one of the main points of Amber's research.

SARAH: You what?

EDWARD: (Despondently) I said Amber thought Lowry returned the compliment by naming the characters in his novel the Llewelyns, after Dylan Thomas's eldest son.

SARAH: But that was your idea! You told her the surname was the name of Dylan's son. She took your idea and then got mad at you for mentioning it?

EDWARD: Whatever. I guess she'd forgotten. (Speaking quickly) Amber was livid. She left in a rush. I called for her to wait, but she ran outside. By this time, it was snowing. She got in the driver's seat. Usually I drive, but I started sweeping snow off the windshield. Then I went around to the passenger side. That's when it happened.

SOUND: Car crashing.

If I'd been standing by Amber, the guy would have seen me. She should have been in the passenger seat.

SARAH: Ed. It was an accident.

EDWARD: I shouldn't have given the paper.

SARAH: What are we going to do?

EDWARD: (Pause) The doctor said you could come with me to the next appointment if you want to, Sarah.

SARAH: We'll see.

TRANSITION: Ukulele flow.

NARRATOR: A beach party at Dollarton, 1946.

VOICES: (Overlapping campfire voices) Look at those stars, I could watch them forever! Throw another log on the fire.

SOUND: Ukulele music.

VOICE: How about a song, Margerie?

MARG: Well, if you insist. This is an oldie goldie. I heard it on the radio this morning. (Sings) *"On a day like today, We pass the time away, Writing Love Letters in the Sand. How you laughed when I cried each time I saw the tide, take our love letters from the sand. Now my poor heart just aches, with ev'ry wave that breaks, over Love Letters in the Sand ..."*

LOWRY: (Shouts) Hell. Look at that SHELL sign, Earle.

BIRNEY: Calm down, man.

LOWRY: At least now that the "S" has burnt out, the name is appropriate. Hell, I hear they're thinking of running another pipeline from Alberta. I should write a little ditty about that. Or maybe you'd like to do it. *"Hell, hell, hell, everything should be swell, swell, swell."*

BIRNEY: (With a laugh) Thanks, but no thanks.

LOWRY: (Laughs good-naturedly) All right, my friend. But you know I admire your work. I wish I were a poet, instead of a plagiarist.

BIRNEY: You aren't a plagiarist.

LOWRY: That's what some people are calling me. *Under The Volcano* is full of symbols used by other writers. I've started a letter to Cape explaining them all.

BIRNEY: Let it go man. It's nothing. Everyone knows about your photographic memory. Remember when you recited a scene from *The Tempest* at that party? You need a holiday.

SOUND: Bracelets jingling.

MARG: (Joining in) That's what I keep telling him.

LOWRY: The constant threat of eviction drives us to distraction. We have to move.

BIRNEY: Have you found a place?

LOWRY: Possibly. Margerie has a friend who lives on Gabriola Island.

BIRNEY: Gabriola, you say?

MARG: Yes! My dear friend, Angela McKee, says there's a cabin for rent near her house, right on the water. She thinks it might be the perfect place for us. There's a ferry from Nanaimo. It's peaceful and quiet. It's got good beaches.

LOWRY: I'm going for a swim. Care to join me, Earle?

BIRNEY: The water's too cold for me! (Calls) Don't stay in too long. (Pause) How is he doing, Margerie?

MARG: He'll be fine. Eating better and exercising. Malcolm, of course, is still a Brit at heart. He loves long-distance swimming. He works and then goes for a swim. Then he writes some more and swims again, all alone. Did he tell you *Under the Volcano* has been accepted?

BIRNEY: He told me he has more work to do.

MARG: I'm going to help him with those proofs and then put them in the mail for him.

BIRNEY: That's a good idea.

MARG: He's afraid to mail it.

BIRNEY: He told me he's done a lot of writing. Is he still drinking?

MARG: (Changing the subject) Did Malcolm tell you we spent a night with

Dylan Thomas in Vancouver? Now, there's a great poet. He and Malc get along famously. Of course they're old friends. All those years Malcolm was writing *Under the Volcano*, Dylan was working on his play. I believe when he renamed it *Under Milkwood*, it was a sign of admiration for Malcolm. Wow! Look at those stars. I could lie on the sand reciting their names all night. (Pause) Oh, here he comes now. (To Lowry) That was a short swim, Malcolm.

LOWRY: I couldn't go in the water.

MARG: What's happened?

LOWRY: It's a ghastly disaster. That SHELL Refinery is going to be the death of us all. There are dead seagulls lying all over the beach. We are going to be poisoned, given enough time.

MARG: There, there. Here, take some vitamins. They'll help you calm down.

SOUND: Pill bottle rattling.

MARG: Just swallow them!

SOUND: Ukulele playing a verse of *Love Letters in the Sand.*

NARRATOR: Now, we're going to break for a short intermission. When you hear this sound (ukulele loud), you'll know it's time to come back.

INTERMISSION

October Ferries to Gabriola

Act Two

SOUND: Loud ukulele flow.

NARRATOR: Welcome back. We now join Jan Gabrial.

JAN: I have to hand it to Margerie. After a few weeks of Malcolm, I got over my fascination with being married to a genius. He couldn't finish things, and if he did, he wouldn't submit them. Margerie must have done it for him. But, Malcolm needed more than a secretary. He needed a mother. Malcolm told me he hated his mother, but he started writing to her after *Under the Volcano* was published.

Of course, after she died, he would have been well off. (Pause) He would have been free to write without money worries. Writing and the simple life were all he wanted. It was the only reason he would cut back on his drinking. But Margerie wouldn't have been satisfied with the simple life. What motivated her to stick with him until he died so mysteriously?

TRANSITION: Bus, ferry horn.

NARRATOR: It's October, 1946. Near the ferry terminal in Nanaimo.

SOUND: Bus arriving.

LOWRY: Driver, could you kindly tell us where we catch the ferry to Gabriola?

DRIVER: Just ahead, near the Bastion. But the Atrevida doesn't run regularly in October.

MARG: We were told there would be a ferry at five o'clock.

DRIVER: It's possible. If you see a line-up of vehicles, ask the drivers.

LOWRY: Thank you. Margerie, let's go to that hotel and see what we can find out. I need a drink.

MARG: And I need to phone Angela and tell her we're coming.

LOWRY: It'll be good to get out of the cold. Although you'll be warm enough.

MARG: I hope you aren't going to start in again about my fur coat. After I received the advance for my last book, I wanted to treat myself.

LOWRY: Arctic skunk! Never mind. I see the ferry docking.

SOUND: Ferry docking.

MARG: Too late to phone. We'll surprise them! I can hardly wait to see our little cottage by the sea.

LOWRY: Paradise regained!

SOUND: Ferry pulling out. Ferry horn.

LOWRY: Let's take a look around. It's a short ride.

MARG: One truck and three cars! That's all, and it's a tight fit.

LOWRY: But lots of walk-ons. They look very smart. Tweed suits and nice coats. Where did they all come from?

MARG: That woman with the shawl around her head doesn't look too well. People are talking to her; they look concerned. That must be her husband.

LOWRY: Oh, and look my darling, the deliverymen are rolling on a washing machine. I'll get you one of those babies.

MARG: Maybe it's for Angela. I can't wait to see her. And meet her husband. We get a taxi to Anderson Lodge. Then, when we're unpacked, we can walk over to their house. They're close by apparently. I've got directions, but it might be dark.

LOWRY: You're shivering. Let's just stay home for the first night.

MARG: Oh, you goof. I want to go out. To see Angela.

SOUND: Ferry departing, horn.

LOWRY: This calls for a celebration. I just got the cap off this bottle.

SOUND: Drinking, glug, glug, glug.

MARG: No, thanks. I don't want to make a bad impression when I arrive. (Pause) Oh, all right. Just one sip.

LOWRY: Give it back. (Laughs)

MARGE: You have to catch me first.

SOUND: Footsteps on metal ferry deck.

LOWRY: Gotcha!

MARG: I give in. It's all yours. But look at that poor woman. What's happened to her?

LOWRY: Apparently, she's had all her teeth out, without anesthetic. I heard them talking about it when I was in the lavatory. The ferry might turn around.

MARG: That's terrible.

LOWRY: She'll be OK if she gets to a doctor right away.

MARG: It's terrible for us! Couldn't they let us off and then turn back. We might not make it. I knew it was too good to be true.

LOWRY: We'll get there. I have it in good confidence that this happens occasionally. The ferry will turn around, let her off in Nanaimo, and then make the crossing back to Gabriola. We'll be there tonight.

SOUND: Ferry horn, three beeps.

MARG: You're in a good mood. Usually you're the pessimistic one.

LOWRY: I'm going to give the husband this gin.

MARG: How kind. Be sure to offer it to his wife also.

SOUND: Male footsteps on metal.

LOWRY: For your wife.

MAN: Thank you sir.

MARG: I see ominous shapes.

LOWRY: (Quoting from *The Tempest*) *"Be not afeared; The isle is full of noises, sounds, and sweet airs, that give delight, and hurt not. Sometimes a thousand twanging instruments will hum about mine ears; and sometimes voices, that, if I then had waked after long sleep, will make me sleep again: and then in dreaming the clouds me thought would open ..."*

MARG: Oh, Malcolm. You are a genius.

LOWRY: "And then in dreaming, the clouds methought would open and riches show, ready to drop upon me; that when I waked, I cried to dream again."

TRANSITION: Ukulele flow.

NARRATOR: The present day. In the cabin on Gabriola.

JAN: I envy them that ferry ride to Gabriola. Malcolm describes it so poetically in his book, *October Ferry to Gabriola*. (Quotes from book) *"The shadow of the mountains had lengthened across the sea, already overpowering the ferryboat, enveloping the Llewelyns as they stood alone at the rail, and reaching out ahead toward Gabriola. Beneath them the sea looked greenish black, then black as India ink, the white bow wave breaking and foaming sternward along its edge then, aft, flattening out like marble."*

SOUND: Keyboarding.

EDWARD: I have to write. It lifts my spirits. Something. A magazine article. Anything would be good. But I can't stop thinking of Lowry. He's my passion—and my punishment.

SOUND: Female footsteps.

SARAH: Forget Lowry! Work on something else. A novel maybe.

EDWARD: A novel? Why not? That would give me something to think about. I should research Lowry's time in jail. I could get thrown in jail.

SARAH: Oh, Edward.

EDWARD: Lowry always wrote. According to this article in *The New Yorker*, he was happily working on *October Ferry to Gabriola* before he died. I believe it. When he was writing, he was happy.

SARAH: So how did he die? Was it death by misadventure, like they said at the inquest? Suicide?

EDWARD: Not suicide. Something inexplicable, an accident or mix-up. I'll never believe it was suicide. If Lowry had planned his own death, he would have first written a fitting opus. He never quit. I shouldn't have quit.

SOUND: Computer ding indicating an email has arrived.

SARAH: Hey, you've got an email from your thesis advisor! She's answering your request for another chance. Do you want to read it or should I?

EDWARD: Read it to me. Please.

SARAH: OK. *"Dear Edward, I can't begin to say how sorry I am for all that happened. I have taken another look at Amber's research and there is no mention of October Ferry to Gabriola, or the idea that Lowry named the Llewelyns after*

Dylan Thomas's son. You were right in your letter."

EDWARD: I can't believe it!

SARAH: It was your idea, not hers. You have to tell them. Sit here and read it. It's your message.

SOUND: Chair being pulled out.

EDWARD: (Reading the email) *"I feel it's unfortunate that two good pieces of research could be lost. It would be a tribute to Amber to have her work come to something, and because you are living on Gabriola, there's an opportunity for you to add new information about the Lowrys to your thesis."* (Pause) Oh man! What do you think, Sarah?

SARAH: I think it's a way for you to move forward, but you have to decide. It has nothing to do with me.

EDWARD: It has everything to do with you. With us!

SARAH: Oh Ed. It would be great if you did it.

EDWARD: I'd like to complete all the unfinished business. Get myself back on my feet. I think this is going to be good for us, Sarah.

SARAH: I can't wait to tell the good news to the Hopes.

TRANSITION: Cheerful ukulele playing *Love Letters in the Sand*.

NARRATOR: October 1946. Anderson Lodge, later renamed Surf Lodge, on Gabriola Island.

SOUND: Male footsteps pacing.

MARG: Oh Malcolm, stop pacing! Surely it's easier to read your manuscript sitting down? (Sigh of contentment) I'm so glad we came to Gabriola.

LOWRY: I am too.

MARG: I've been thinking about our idea for a short story describing our ferry ride to Gabriola. I've made some notes.

LOWRY: I've got a few notes also.

MARG: I know. I took a peek at them.

LOWRY: That's a sneaky thing to do.

MARG: It looks like *October Ferry* is a long story already.

LOWRY: Maybe we shouldn't write it together.

MARG: We agreed to work on it together. Face it, Malcolm. If we don't, it'll never get done. (Sighs) Let's go and look at that little cabin on Seagirt Road. We don't need to work. We're just killing time until we get the galley proofs from Jonathan Cape.

LOWRY: There's a boat down there. We can row out to Entrance Island.

MARG: And we can mail my letter. I've written to Douglas Day to say I've started *The Last Twist of the Knife*. I've a great idea. The wife gives her husband a whole handful of pills.

LOWRY: That's just twaddle!

MARG: He thinks they're vitamins. Then she gives him a glass of over-proof rum.

LOWRY: Not gin, my darling?

MARG: Then, at the inquest, she is all doe-eyed and innocent, knowing that nothing will happen to her. The doctor prescribed the pills.

LOWRY: (Menacingly) Margerie.

SOUND: Pill bottle rattling.

LOWRY: Just shut up or I'll strangle you!

MARG: You shut up, or I'll ...

SOUND: Knocking on door, door opens.

SERVANT: Good Morning, Mrs. Lowry. Here's your wash water.

MARG: I hope it's hot this time.

SERVANT: Yes it is. Here's a letter also.

MARG: Thank you. Oh, it's from our publisher. My husband is about to have his book published. It's a masterpiece.

SERVANT: I'm sure it is.

LOWRY: You are very kind. Very kind indeed. What a luxury to have our water delivered to the door. At our old place, I used to have to walk every evening to a spring to collect water in an old canister.

MARG: We were roughing it there, but it was our choice, of course.

SERVANT: I'm sure it was.

SOUND: Envelope being ripped open. Paper being pulled out.

MARG: Wow!

LOWRY: Now what?

SOUND: Paper rustling.

MARG: (Excitedly) Oh my goodness, a formal invitation. It's Jonathan Cape suggesting we do a book tour in Europe after the launch of *Under the Volcano*.

LOWRY: It isn't even out yet. I don't like counting my chickens before they hatch. I don't like talking about it. It's bad luck. Besides, I hate going to literary gatherings.

MARG: It would only be for a few days.

LOWRY: Do we have to go? Just when we've found a place to settle?

MARG: We can come back. It'll be good for us to get away. And they'll be picking up the tab. Our friends will be so impressed. I always did think Earle Birney just wanted to be friends with us because you are famous.

LOWRY: You've got it all wrong, Margerie.

TRANSITION: Seagulls squawking.

NARRATOR: The cabin on Gabriola in [today's year].

SOUND: Female footsteps.

SOUND: Sarah humming.

SARAH: (Singing) *"On a day like today, we passed the time away ..."*

SOUND: Door opening.

SARAH: Oh Ed, you should see the roses. How's it going?

EDWARD: Good. I'm taking a break. You know it's touching to read about the postcards Lowry sent back from Europe. Malcolm wrote to Angela saying ...

LOWRY: They talk about the Blue Danube. It doesn't compare with the waters of

Gabriola. It is so much nicer on Gabriola than here.

EDWARD: The difficult thing is the Lowrys were always on the go. My readers will be dizzy. Now I have to get the Lowrys to England for the last months before Malcolm's death.

SARAH: You think Margerie did him in, don't you?

EDWARD: What do you think? "Death by misadventure" was all they said at the inquest.

SARAH: It was one or the other. If she didn't kill him, he'd have killed her. What I can't believe is his tombstone. All Margerie put on it was his name and the dates. "Malcolm Lowry (1909-1957)." Not even "In Loving Memory," or "A Great Writer."

EDWARD: That's a good point. Margerie was always telling people he was a genius. Well, at least she convinced the clergy it wasn't suicide and got him accepted into the church graveyard.

SARAH: But you said only seven people attended his funeral. That's sad.

EDWARD: Yeah, it is sad. Let's go for a walk. I'd like to run an idea by you.

SOUND: Footsteps. Door opens. Sea lions barking.

EDWARD: Honey, look! The whole world is walking down our road.

SARAH: They're going to watch the sunset. They call it the Magic Mile. Oh, Ed. Wouldn't it be magical if the Lowrys had returned? If they were still here? Imagine if we could meet them!

SOUND: Tinkling bell to signal a shift to an imaginary world.

EDWARD: Yes, imagine! Did you hear the sea lions barking? It's amazing.

SOUND: Sea lions barking. Footsteps on gravel.

MARG: (Calls loudly) Hey, you two. Where have you been? We haven't seen you in a while!

SARAH: Hello. Yes, it's been quite a while since we've seen you.

MARG: We haven't been out and about much. We've been so busy! We just found out from one of my fans that my latest novel was published without the final chapter! I'm going to give my publisher a piece of my mind.

LOWRY: Maybe it's a good thing the last chapter was missing! The heroine kills off her husband.

MARG: Oh, you goof!

LOWRY: How are you folks doing?

EDWARD: Fine, thanks. We're just out to enjoy the view.

MARG: Oh, maybe you'd like to join us up on the bluff later on. I'll bring a thermos of tea and we can look at the stars.

LOWRY: Yes, do. It would be very nice, Sarah, if you brought that ukulele of yours.

SARAH: I'd love to! I feel a song coming on.

SOUND: Ukulele sting.

LOWRY: So, we'll see you later then?

MARG: Oh, no! I just remembered we have to meet friends tonight.

EDWARD: Then we'll hope to see you another time.

LOWRY: I hope so, too. Let's shake on it. (Lowry shaking hands with Sarah and Edward) Sarah ... Edward.

EDWARD: Keep writing.

LOWRY: *Sursum corda*.

MARG: (Condescendingly) That's Latin for lift up your hearts.

EDWARD: Yes, I know.

MARG: Cheerio, kids!

TRANSITION: *Rule Britannia* plus sound of Big Ben striking.

NARRATOR: After the war, Malcolm and Margerie went into couple's therapy.

British psychiatrists met with them in England in an effort to try to help them with their troubles. Malcolm wasn't drinking, and by all accounts they were happy in a little cottage in Ripe. Malcolm had started writing again, and as it often happened, he seemed in better shape than Margerie. Maybe that's what bothered her.

Dr.#1: Good afternoon, Doctor. The Lowrys will be here any minute. Apparently they have seen other psychiatrists in Europe.

Dr.#2: Yes. You said they were both hospitalized in Italy?

Dr.#1: He tried to strangle her. He got very violent.

Dr.#2: Really? Right in the hospital?

Dr.#1: Yes. More than once.

Dr.#2: Imagine. Why did she stick with him?

Dr.#1: (Shrugs) Well, according to the reports, Lowry had gone through aversion therapy and quit drinking.

Dr.#2: (Footsteps) Interesting.

Dr.#1: They're here now. I'll bring them in.

SOUND: Door opens. Footsteps entering room. Door closes.

Dr.#2: Hello. Have a seat. We'd like to start by having you fill us in on what's been happening with you over the last year.

MARG: Well. You must know my husband is a famous novelist. We recently toured all over Europe to promote his new book, *Under the Volcano*. Rome, Paris, you name it. Everywhere except where I wanted to go. To Switzerland, to see Carl Jung. If only Malcolm had been nicer to his mother, she would have paid for it. I went by myself to ask her for the money. She said she was proud of Malcolm but didn't give me a penny.

SOUND: Bracelets jingling.

LOWRY: My mother passed away recently and money isn't an issue.

MARG: It's too late now!

Dr.#1: You were both hospitalized in Paris.

MARG: And in Rome! The guard at my door fell asleep and Malcolm tried to strangle me.

Dr.#1: Then, what did you do?

MARG: Well, after a day or two, Malcolm settled down and I checked him out.

Dr.#1: You were advised to leave him.

MARG: How could I? I'd have nothing. No money. Not even the rights to his books.

LOWRY: I know I can control my violent spells. I'm depressed, but now and again I go crazy. Especially when I've been drinking.

Dr.#2: But you have that under control since the aversion therapy?

LOWRY: Yes. And I've been writing. Rewriting and editing a new novel. When

I'm finished, *October Ferry to Gabriola* will be equal to *Under the Volcano*. If I can keep on at this pace, I'll finish it.

MARG: He never finishes anything. He always rewrites everything. Sometimes I wish he'd just drop dead!

Dr.#1: You've been traveling a lot. That must be tiring.

MARG: Oh, I thrive on it. But Malcolm hasn't been all that interested. And now I'm afraid I have a fatal disease. I don't want to tell Malcolm about it. I don't think he can manage on his own.

LOWRY: (To Dr.#2) Since Margerie hasn't been feeling well, I've had to pull up my socks.

MARG: He doesn't even wear socks. I have to tie his shoes for him.

LOWRY: She's been sleeping a lot. She doesn't even know what's been happening in Hungary. She slept through the revolution.

Dr.#2: Do you have any ideas for working your way out of these problems?

LOWRY: If only we could communicate more effectively.

Dr.#1: Margerie, I think you need a good rest.

MARG: I can't rest with him around.

Dr.#1: This is only our first meeting, but we believe we can help you.

Dr.#2: We're proposing that you, Margerie, stay here at the hospital for tests.

Dr.#1: And Malcolm, we understand you know a few people in Ripe and there's a nice cottage for you to stay in.

LOWRY: Yes, there is. And there's a rectory where I can write. I've still got plenty to do on *October Ferry to Gabriola*.

MARG: Will you write to me, Malcolm? (She starts to cry.)

SOUND: *Writing Love Letters in the Sand* ...

LOWRY: There, there my darling. It will only be for a few days until we start a new life together in Ripe.

SOUND: Kissing.

TRANSITION: Stravinsky opera music.

NARRATOR: It is 1957. A bedroom in Ripe. Margerie and Malcolm are listening to a Stravinsky opera on the radio.

SOUND: Stravinsky opera.

MARG: Turn that radio down!

SOUND: Music gets louder.

LOWRY: I'm listening to this opera and I want it loud.

SOUND: Volume increases.

MARG: But Mrs. Mason might be sleeping. I'm turning it down.

SOUND: Volume goes down. Then up.

LOWRY: To hell with the old lady!

SOUND: Radio being turned off.

MARG: Let's not fight. You're home, after so many years. I'm sorry. We shouldn't have gone to the pub. I'm sure old lady Mason will hear us. (Putting on an English accent) "Oh love, you had us all worried there. I wanted to run over to see if I could be of help." Well, I'll just go next door and borrow a bit of tea. It'll be good to reassure her that we're all right.

We had a little lovers' spat that's all. (Margerie changes her tone) You English and your "cup o' tea". What's wrong with a good cup of coffee!

LOWRY: Just go if you're going!

SOUND: Glass being thrown. Glass breaking. Lowry falls.

LOWRY: I can't get up! (Pause) Margerie? Help me!

SOUND: Door opens, female footsteps exiting, door closes.

LOWRY: Margerie!

SOUND: Pill bottle rattling.

LOWRY: Groans.

SOUND: Beat of silence.

SOUND: Rapid, overlapping voices.

SARAH: We're honeymooners!

EDWARD: I don't like honeymoons.

MARG: I hate being poor.

JAN: I got a job in a dancehall in New York.

LOWRY: They put me in jail for no reason.

MARG: Get up, you drunk!

EDWARD: We're going to Paradise.

JAN: I've had enough!

EDWARD: I don't want to be a zombie.

MARG: You didn't even tell your father we were married.

LOWRY: My old man sent me off to sea in a limousine.

JAN: The patients were crazy. I got him out.

LOWRY: You gold-digging money-grabber.

MARG: I'd love to see those volcanoes.

LOWRY: I couldn't stop my own house from burning down!

MARG: Just look at the stars!

ALL: (Naming the stars) Capella, Fomalhaut, Algol, Mira.

EDWARD: We at Jonathan Cape will publish *Under the Volcano* as is. It is not tedious.

MARG: *Au-Dessous du Volcan!* That's what they called it in France.

JAN: He read my diary.

MARG: Tell her to go to hell!

LOWRY: Who cares about the old lady! I'm listening to this opera. Loud.

JAN: Promise you won't drink.

MARG: We shouldn't have gone to the pub.

LOWRY: Money isn't everything.

EDWARD: The £20,000 pounds after his mother's death came too late.

MARG: It's only vitamins.

LOWRY: I'm not a quitter!

ALL: He choked on his own vomit. It was suicide. No it wasn't. He died playing the ukulele. He was a genius.

LOWRY: For your wife, Sir. Keep the bottle.

MARG: Cheerio, kids. We're on our way.

LOWRY: Sersum corda.

SOUND: Beat of silence.

SOUND: Ferry fog horn.

LOWRY: I wasn't all bad! Margerie, I need you. Help me!

SOUND: Opera music. Music ends. Seagulls.

BLACKOUT

About the Author

Charlotte Cameron finds plays an excellent vehicle to retell important stories. Her two other plays, *No Gun for Annie* (2000) and *Running: The Alex Decoteau Story* (Fictive Press, 2014), also portray real people: Annie Jackson, Canada's first policewoman, and aboriginal World War I hero, Alex Decoteau.

She has also written profiles for Legacy Magazine and articles for Western Living Magazine, BC BookWorld and Canada's History.

Charlotte lives with her husband on Gabriola Island, British Columbia.

Visit Charlotte at fictivepress.com/charlotte-cameron.htm.

Acknowledgements

I would like to thank my friend, Morri Mostow, for editing and publishing this play. As always, she is meticulous and insightful. Her cover is inspired, with images of two ferries to suit the title.

I want to thank my husband, Tom Cameron, for his love and encouragement. He promoted the play enthusiastically, designed the poster, tickets and program for the Surf Lodge performances in October 2016. His proofreading, photographs and technical support are much appreciated. Travelling with him, looking for Lowry locations in British Columbia and Mexico, was a delight.

Special thanks to Alan Twigg for encouraging writers with his publication, *BC BookWorld*. Thanks also for his article about the 70th anniversary celebration of Malcolm Lowry's visit to Gabriola Island (*BC BookWorld*, Spring 2016). I'm thrilled that *October Ferries to Gabriola* was performed in October 2016 at Surf Lodge, which is No. 35 on *BC BookWorld*'s "Literary Map of BC."

I'm grateful to Phyllis Reeve for the foreword. Phyllis and her husband, the late Ted Reeve, gave me advice and encouragement with various versions of the play.

Russell Kilde and Garry Davey helped me get started on the play, which was first presented at the original Roxy Theatre in 2009. Thanks to Naomi Beth Wakan for her enthusiastic comments after the first production, and for her book blurb; to Hilary Peach for including the play in the 2010 Seventh Annual Poetry Gabriola Festival at Dragon's Lodge; and to Gloria Filax for programming a staged reading at the 2013 Island Studies Conference at The Haven.

In 2016, many groups participated in the 70th anniversary celebration of Malcolm Lowry's visit to Gabriola. Thanks to Gloria Hatfield of Pages Resort & Marina Bookstore, The Gabriola Historical & Museum Society, Poetry Gabriola Society, the Gabriola branch of Vancouver Island Regional Library, Friends of the Library, the Gabriola Arts Council, and the Gabriola Ferry Advisory Committee for promoting the anniversary celebration.

Thanks to Ivan Bulic from The Gabriola Historical & Museum Society and his committee for organizing the 2016 Lowry celebration and for preparing the Malcolm Lowry historical plaque, which is now affixed to the exterior wall of the Gabriola ferry terminal in Nanaimo.

Gabriolans Jennifer Nash and John Capon provided new information for an historical perspective. John Capon showed me various places Malcolm and Margerie would have visited near Berry Point Road and shared the memories of Margerie Lowry's friend, Angela McKee, and her husband, Alfred McKee.

Sheryl Salloum did an incredible service to the story in her book *Malcolm Lowry: Vancouver Days* (Harbour Publishing Co. Ltd., 1987). Thanks to Sheryl for writing the book blurb and for attending the 2016 Lowry celebration along with her husband and colleagues from Vancouver.

Thanks also to Sherrill Grace, a world-renowned Lowry expert, who launched the 2016 Lowry celebration with an excellent, enthusiastically received talk.

Gloria Levi, who lived near the Lowrys at Dollarton in the 1950s, graciously agreed to be interviewed by Wendy Strachan. The video of this interview, produced by Richard Strachan, ran continuously in the Gabriola library on October 5, 2016. Levi described Malcolm Lowry as a kind, caring person, whose friends respected him as a writer and individual.

Hats off to the fabulous cast for the premiere performance of the play on October 2 and 3, 2016, at Surf Lodge. Drew Staniland, Kathy McIntyre, Chris Jans, Tina Jones and David Botten made this radio play come alive. I am thrilled by the positive feedback I've received since these two performances.

Thanks to the helpful staff at the University of British Columbia's Rare Books and Special Collections. It was exciting to be able to handle actual Lowry artifacts.

I'm also grateful for the encouragement I've received from family, friends and Gabriolans.

CPSIA information can be obtained
at www.ICGtesting.com
Printed in the USA
LVHW091245290821
696379LV00004B/209